The Manhattan Bridge, New York

4413

Spider-Man...

Where are you?

THE MONEY THING

Sean McKeever — Writer | Takeshi Miyazawa — Pencils | Norman Lee — Inks | Christina Strain — Colors | Virtual Calligraphy's Randy Gentile — Letters | MacKenzie Cadenhead — Editor | C.B. Cebulski — Consulting Editor | Joe Quesada — Chief | Dan Buckley — Publisher

Special Thanks to David Gabriel

VISIT US AT

www.abdopub.com

Spotlight, a division of ABDO Publishing Company Inc., is the school and library distributor of the Marvel Entertainment books.

Library bound edition © 2006

Library of Congress Cataloging-in-Publication Data

The Money Thing

ISBN 1-59961-038-8   (Reinforced Library Bound Edition)

All Spotlight books are reinforced library binding and manufactured in the United States of America

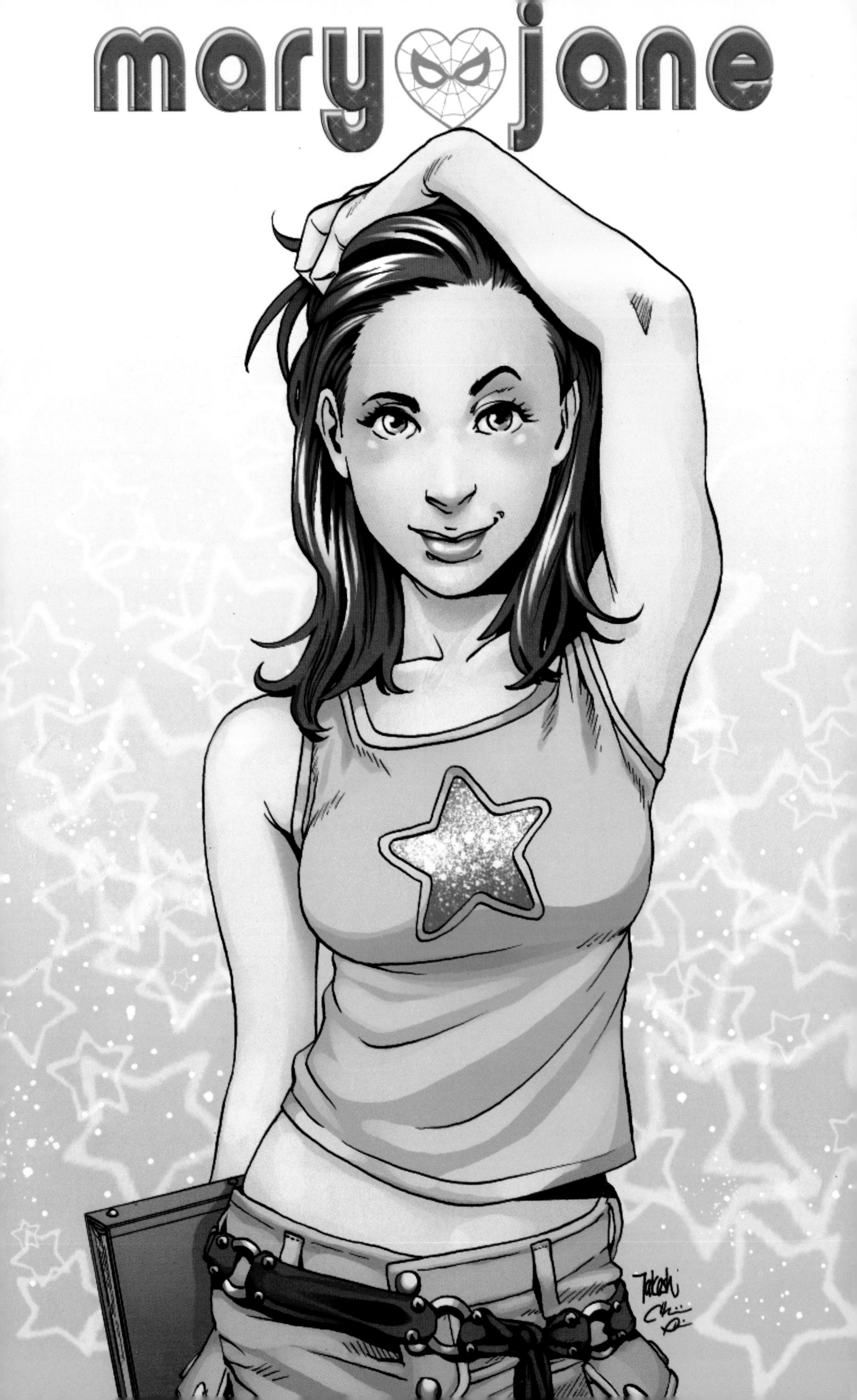
mary jane

FASHION PLUS

Ooh! What about *this* one?

Yeah, it's nice.

Nice? *Mary Jane*, I've picked out the twelve most *stellar* outfits *in* this place, and *nice* is the best you can do?

Pff. Nice. A birthday card from an *aunt* is "nice"...

Liz, don't you think these are all a little--

--expensive?

Skimpy? Sexy? Decadent?

I dunno...maybe I shouldn't *go*...

Maybe *you*--?

Yeah, uh-huh. And maybe *I* shouldn't have a hot, trophy boyfriend.

It's just--

I've been looking *all over* for him; but...I can't *find* him.

Uh...did I *skip* a page somewhere? Him *who*?

You know...

...Spider-Man?

Oh. Oh, wow.

You were *serious* about all that?

Well...

MJ, he's a *super hero*, not a *Homecoming date.*

I mean, come on! What-- would he wear a *suit jacket* over his red-and-blue undies?

For all you know he could be some creepy *old* dude. Seriously.

$40

He's not. He's our age. I actually *spoke* to him, remember?

Tch. Oh, sweetie...

What about *Harry?* I mean, you guys *are* dating--

Yeah, but Harry's just not--

Harry's a *friend,* Liz.

He's just a friend.

MJ, this has been--

I mean, spending time with you like this...it's just been *really* cool. Really.

Thanks, Harry.

Hey, *speaking* of which, uh...you know, *Homecoming's* not that far aw--

Wow.

Would you look at that *view*?

It's really **something,** isn't it? I don't think I could ever get tired of watching the water **move** like that, you know?

It's so...I dunno, **liberating.**

Yeah...

It **is** amazing, isn't it?

Uh-huh...

Two, please. Thanks.

Hey, MJ, you know that **movie** you've been talking about starts this Friday...

Oh, yeah? That's cool...I didn't...

Thanks. Here you go.

Keep the change.

Fifteen dollars, please.

Day after Maniana   1:2
SHRAK   1:10 3:10 5:1
Chill Will   1:30 4:40 7:3
Barry Podder 2:30 5:4
Been Saved?   1:10 3:3
Mean Boys   12:00 2:00
ronica   ittec 12:

Thank you, sir.

Hhh...

I need a job.

So...okay, *Mary*, in what way--

Mary Jane.

Uh-huh.

So, in what way do you feel you're *ideal* for this position?

Oh!

Well, I...

I'm a hard worker. I have-- at least I *think* I have--a very outgoing personality, and I always try to be *really* nice to people. I always put my best foot forward.

Oh, and I'm *totally* a team player.

Uh-huh.

And what, then, would you say is your biggest weakness?

Weakness? Um...

I sometimes work *too* hard? Heh...

Welcome to *Hungry Hippo's™,* home of the *Happy Hungry Hippo Harvest®!*

Would you like to try a *Double-Bacon Hippo with Cheese®?*

Good luck, Mary. I *know* you'll do great!

Thank you, Mr. Muntz.

Did you want the *Harvest,* or just the sandwich?

Gnehh...!

If I *wanted* the *Harvest,* I would have *asked* for the *Harvest!*

Where's this woman's *Chicken Hippo®,* no bun, extra cheese, extra mayo? She's been waiting *ten minutes!*

Hey, it ain't *my* problem...

Watch it! She's *crazy!*

You'll singe us *all!*

Can you tell me--

Just one moment, ple--

Excuse me. I ordered a *Quarter-Pound Hippo Classic®* with *the works.* This is a *Quarter-Pound Neo Hippo®* with cheese and *ketchup.*

Ohmygosh, sir, I'm *so sorry.* I--

Hey, are you gonna take *my* order or what?

mnn...?

Miss Watson.

It would *appear* that your level of *alertness* in this class is declining as *steadily* as your *grades* are of late.

Don't let me catch you napping in here *again.*

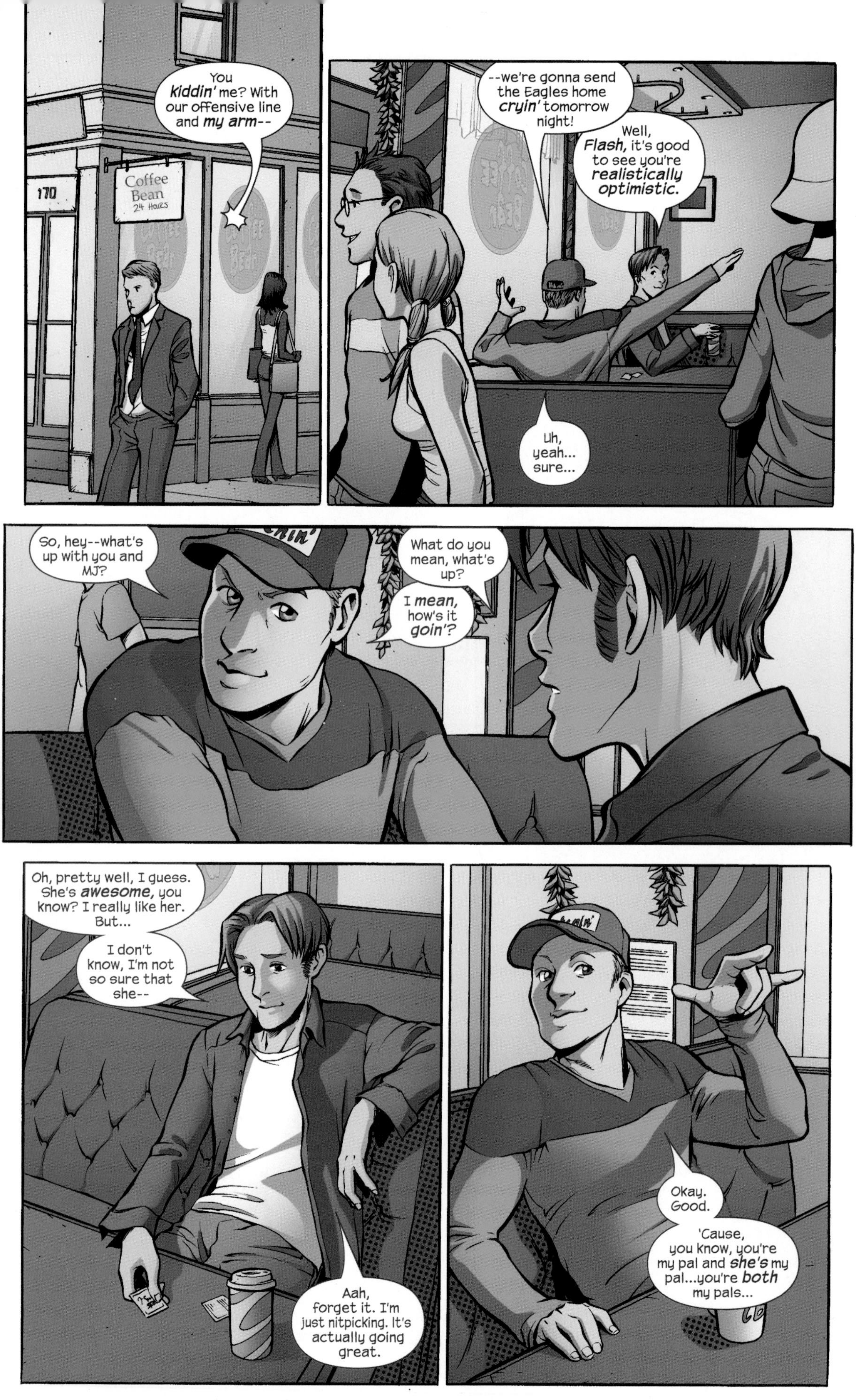

You kiddin' me? With our offensive line and my arm--
170
Coffee Bean 24 Hours
--we're gonna send the Eagles home cryin' tomorrow night!
Well, Flash, it's good to see you're realistically optimistic.
Uh, yeah... sure...
So, hey--what's up with you and MJ?
What do you mean, what's up?
I mean, how's it goin'?
Oh, pretty well, I guess. She's awesome, you know? I really like her. But...
I don't know, I'm not so sure that she--
Aah, forget it. I'm just nitpicking. It's actually going great.
Okay. Good.
'Cause, you know, you're my pal and she's my pal...you're both my pals...

...but if you do *anything* to hurt her, I *swear* I'll--

Hey, what's *up*, Harry? I--

Boo!

That's right-- *take a hike*, Puny Parker. Let the *men* talk, okay?

Flash...

What?

Peter's a good guy... I don't see why you--

MMAH!

What's up, studly?

What're you two *talking* about?

Just stuff and... stuff...

Ooh. *Riveting.*

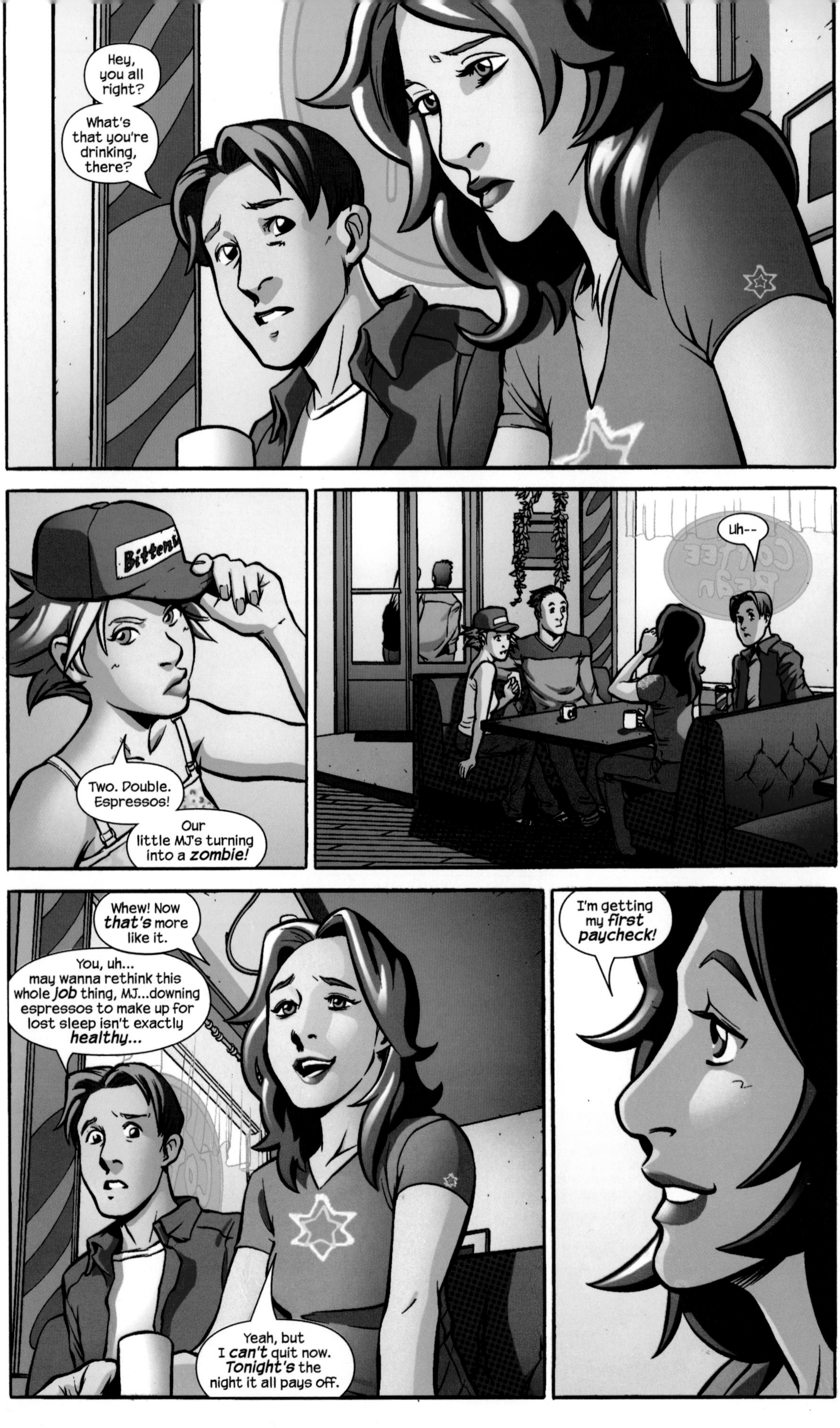

Hey, you all right?
What's that you're drinking, there?
Bittens
Two. Double. Espressos!
Our little MJ's turning into a *zombie!*
Uh--
Whew! Now *that's* more like it.
You, uh... may wanna rethink this whole *job* thing, MJ...downing espressos to make up for lost sleep isn't exactly *healthy...*
Yeah, but I *can't* quit now. *Tonight's* the night it all pays off.
I'm getting my *first paycheck!*

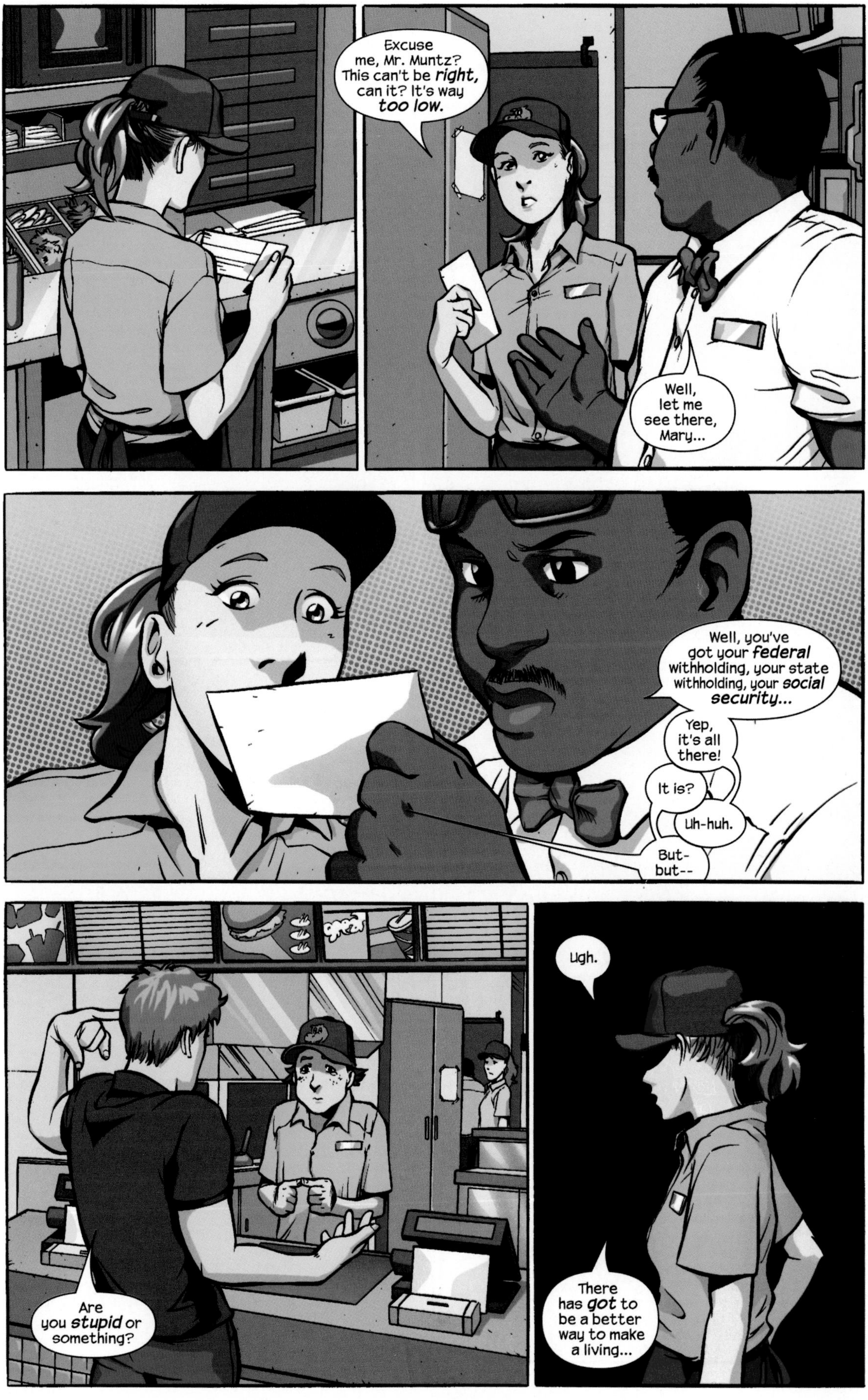
Excuse me, Mr. Muntz? This can't be right, can it? It's way too low.
Well, let me see there, Mary...
Well, you've got your federal withholding, your state withholding, your social security...
Yep, it's all there!
It is?
Uh-huh.
But-but--
Are you stupid or something?
Ugh.
There has got to be a better way to make a living...

Oh, don't rent that one. That one *bites.*

And that other one, too.

--and if you want *any* sort of tip, you'll take this travesty *back* to the chef and tell him it tastes like a *salty, wet sock.*

Yes? Is this Dr. Sumerak for Mr. Oberlander?

...

Ohh...! Dr. Oberlander for Mr. Hollenbach! Okay. And this was regarding...?

...

Hello? I didn't hang up on you *again,* did I?

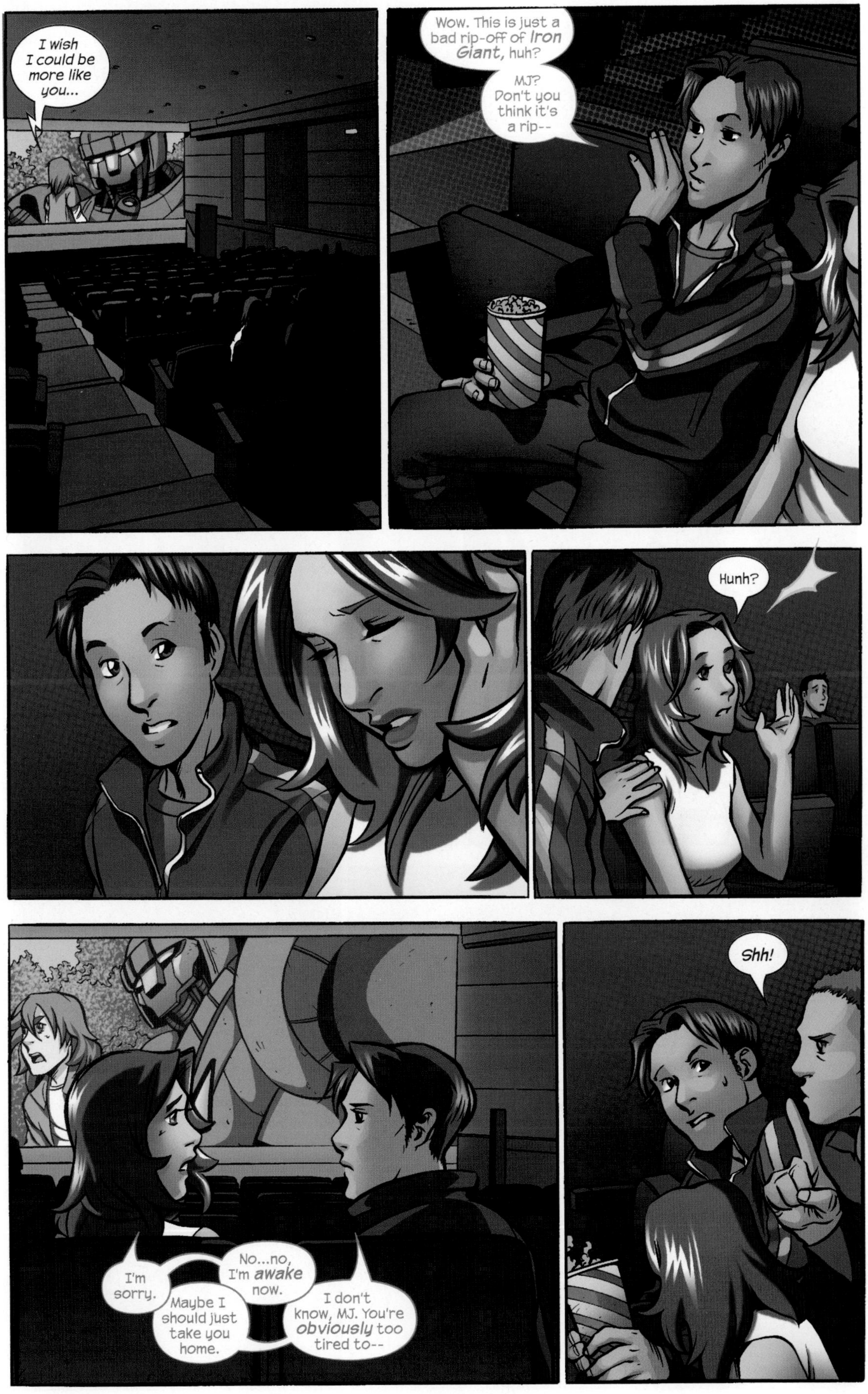
I wish I could be more like you...
Wow. This is just a bad rip-off of Iron Giant, huh?
MJ? Don't you think it's a rip--
Hunh?
I'm sorry.
No...no, I'm awake now.
Maybe I should just take you home.
I don't know, MJ. You're obviously too tired to--
Shh!

You know, this whole *job* thing is really putting a big, rainy *cloud* over your social life.

I know...

It's like you're not the same *MJ* anymore. Always tired, always *distant*...

Yeah, I know...

...but I'm sure that once I find that *one job* that's *perfect* for me, this *won't* be a big deal anymore.

Mary Jane...you *don't* have to do this because of me, you know.

What're you talking about?

I know it bothers you, but I don't *mind* paying for stuff. I can *afford* to take you out, so--

Oh, hey! Look!

Spider-Man:

Can You **Trust** Him?

Read the D_ Bugle

Mr. Limke?

Hi. You wanted to see me?

Yeah. Come on in.

Miss Watson, what's up?

What... what do you mean?

I hear you've been catching a fair number of *Zs* in class. And I *hear* it's started to affect your *grades*.

So, what's up?

I dunno.

You know, I've chatted with *ten* students today, and they *all* had the same answer?

That "I dunno" bug sure does get *around* this place, doesn't it?

I guess...I guess I've been--

I took a job? Well, I've taken a *few* different jobs, but...

So, I guess, you know...that's why I've been kinda tired in class.

How's your *mom* doing? She's still employed?

Oh, yeah, she's still *working* and stuff...it's just that--

You know, she *makes* enough to--

Actually, I'm not really comfortable talking about that.

That's cool--I understand. Just remember, what we talk about here *stays* here, same as always.

You know, you're not alone. You have fellow students putting in *forty-hour work weeks* just to make ends meet.

Really?

Mm-hmm. And, while it does appear to work fine for *some* of them, others find their grades *suffering* for it. Some of them are *failing*.

Heh...but who am I to tell them *learning* is more important than *food*, or a *roof* over their heads, right?

What you should *ask* yourself, Miss Watson, is if what you're doing is making ends meet...

...or if it's something else.

Well, today's gonna be my last day, anyway, so--

You know, there *are* other options. You don't have to *quit*--

Nah, it's okay...I mean, every job I *got*, either I wasn't any *good* at it, or I completely *hated* it.

I don't ever want to clean another filthy hotel room again.

I just wanted to be able to, you know, *do* stuff with my friends and not feel--

I don't want someone else or some other... *factor* to be in control of what I can or can't do.

I dunno...

...I thought money was supposed to make everything *easier*.

Tch...

See ya 'round, Homecoming dress...

It would've been fun.

WOW, nice choice!

Mnn?

Oh. Thanks.

That color's *great* for you! You should *really* try it on...

Oh. Oh, no.

I can't.

Of *course* you can! You're gonna look *amazing.* This is for *Homecoming,* right?

Well, yeah, but actually, I was just--

I mean, I wasn't really planning on--

Heh...

You know, I just can't really afford it, so...

Oh.

We do have a *layaway plan* that--

No, I mean, really I just don't--

I don't have the money. But thanks.

Well, you *know...*

...you seem like a sweet girl, and one of my *salespeople* just went on *maternity leave.*

I was going to just *make do* without a replacement, but I *tell* ya, it's just *not* the same without a *second body* in here.

It's not a lot of *hours*, I'm afraid...

...but if you come in a few hours after school every couple days and help out, I'll *make sure* you have enough to buy that dress for Homecoming.

So? What do you think?

I think...

I think I'd like to put this on layaway, please.